The story of
DANIEL

by LUCY DIAMOND
with illustrations by KENNETH INNS

Ladybird Books Loughborough

THE STORY OF DANIEL

Six hundred years before Jesus was born, the greatest king of the East was Nebuchadnezzar the Chaldean.

He had conquered Babylonia and taken the city of Babylon for his capital. This city he made beautiful with temples and a splendid palace which, with its " hanging gardens " on high terraces, was one of the wonders of the ancient world.

Part of his vast Chaldean empire was the Jewish land of Judah.

But Jehoiakim, who reigned in Jerusalem, rebelled against his overlord. Jehoiakim was a wicked king, and when Nebuchadnezzar marched in anger against Jerusalem, " God gave Jehoiakim into his hand."

Nebuchadnezzar destroyed the royal city, captured the king and many of his people, and seized part of the gold and silver vessels from the Temple of the Lord.

Nebuchadnezzar returned to Babylon with hundreds of Jewish prisoners, and the sacred gold and silver vessels which he placed in the temple of his heathen god.

Then he called Ashpenaz, the Master of his Household.

" Some of these children of Israel are princes and nobles," he said. " Choose out those who are bright and good-looking, and able to study the language and wisdom of the Chaldeans—boys worthy to stand in my palace."

" For three years they shall have meat and wine from my own table, that they may be well fed. At the end of that time you shall bring them before me."

Ashpenaz obeyed—and among the boys he chose were Daniel and his three friends, whose Chaldean names were Shadrach, Meshach, and Abed-nego.

Each day the king sent the boys meat and wine from his table.

But Daniel said to his friends, " By God's law this heathen meat is forbidden. We must not eat it."

He asked the steward who waited on them if they might have vegetables to eat and water to drink, instead of the king's meat and wine.

" But you will grow thin and pale," the man replied. " Then the king will be angry and punish me."

" May we try for ten days," Daniel pleaded. The steward agreed, and for ten days the friends ate plain food and drank water. Their faces grew fresh and rosy, and they were stronger than the boys who had eaten the king's meat.

So the steward let the four friends eat as the law of their God allowed.

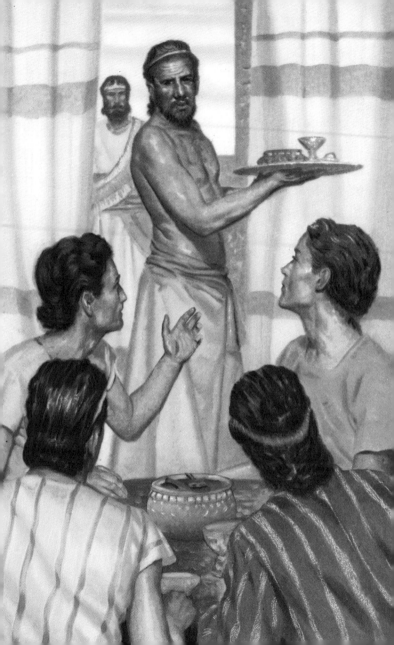

Now these four youths faithfully studied the strange language and wisdom of the Chaldeans, and God gave them knowledge and skill in learning, and Daniel had understanding in all visions and dreams.

At last the time came for Ashpenaz to bring his pupils in before the king.

Nebuchadnezzar talked with them and found that they could now understand his words, and answer him in his own tongue.

He asked them many questions, and was pleased to see how much they had learned.

But among them all he found none so good as Daniel and his three friends. In every way they were ten times better than all the magicians and wise men in his realm.

So the king chose them to attend him in his palace.

One night Nebuchadnezzar had a strange dream. When he awoke he was troubled— yet he could not remember why.

He had forgotten his dream.

He called his wise men and magicians.

" I have dreamed a dream," he said. " I am worried about it."

" Tell us the dream," they answered, " and we will soon tell you what it means."

" I have forgotten it," the king told them impatiently. " Tell me what it was, and what it means, or I will punish you. If you make this thing clear to me, I will give you riches and honours."

The wise men grew anxious.

" There is no one on earth who can do this," they pleaded. " Only the gods can tell you your dream."

Then Nebuchadnezzar was furious.

" If you cannot tell me the dream," he raged, " then how can you truly show its meaning! You will only tell me lies."

In his anger, Nebuchadnezzar ordered all the wise men of Babylon to be destroyed. So the soldiers went to find Daniel and his friends to kill them.

" Why is this? " Daniel asked their captain. When the captain of the guard explained, Daniel hurried to the palace.

" O king," he begged, " do not destroy your wise men. Give me time, and I will show you the dream and its meaning."

So the king waited, and Daniel went back to his house. There he and his friends prayed to God to show them this secret, so that they, with all the wise men of Babylon, should not be destroyed.

Their prayer was answered. The king's dream was shown to Daniel in a vision of the night.

How joyfully the four friends gave thanks to God!

Then Daniel went to the Captain of the guard. " Bring me in before the king," he said. " I will now show him his dream and its meaning."

The Captain hurried to take Daniel before the king.

" O king," he cried, " I have found a man— one of the captives of Judah. He will tell you your dream."

" Can you really do this? " Nebuchad-nezzar asked Daniel.

" No man on earth can tell you a dream you have forgotten," Daniel answered. " But there is a God in heaven Who knows all things. He has shown me the secret in a vision.

" This is your dream, O king. You saw a great, shining image—huge and terrible."

" Its head was of fine gold, its body and limbs of silver and brass and iron, and its feet of clay and iron."

" Then a stone was cut out without hands, and the stone struck the image upon its feet—and it fell with a crash."

" The splendid image lay broken into pieces, which the wind carried away until there was nothing left."

" But the stone which struck the image became a great mountain, and it filled all the earth."

" Now we will show you the meaning of the dream to you, O Nebuchadnezzar, king of kings, to whom the God of Heaven has given the kingdom, the power and the glory."

18

"God has given you great dominions, and made you ruler over them. You are the head of fine gold."

"But after you, other kingdoms shall rise up—some good and strong like the silver and brass and iron—but others divided, like the iron and clay, which do not mix, and so are weak and easily broken."

"You saw a stone cut without hands which broke in pieces the iron, the brass, the clay, the silver and the gold."

"That is the greatest kingdom of all, which the God of heaven shall set up. It shall never be destroyed. It shall stand for ever."

Thus, long ago, the coming of the Lord Jesus and the glory of His Kingdom was foretold to the greatest king of the East.

As Daniel finished speaking, Nebuchadnezzar fell on his face to worship him. But Daniel said:

" It is the God of Heaven—not I—who has shown you what shall happen in the days to come."

The king answered humbly.

" Truly your God is the God of gods and the Lord of kings, seeing that He has made you able to tell me these secret things."

Then the king honoured Daniel, and gave him many rich gifts. He made him ruler over all the province of Babylon, and chief governor of all his wise men.

But Daniel did not forget his friends.

He told Nebuchadnezzar about them, and the king gave Shadrach, Meshach and Abed-nego other posts as rulers in Babylon.

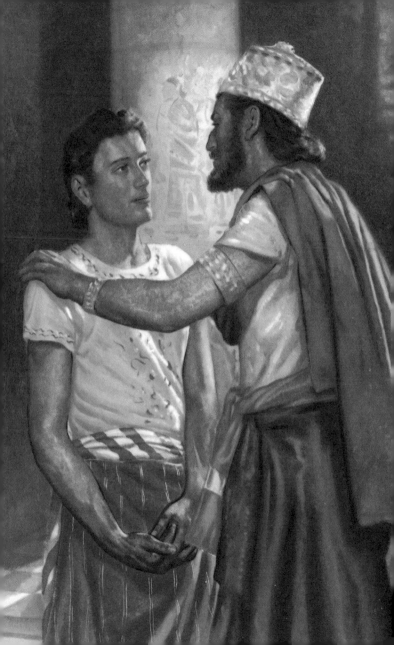

So the four young Jewish captives were greatly honoured, but Daniel was nearest to the king, who kept him constantly at his court.

All through Nebuchadnezzar's long reign Daniel remained his most trusted adviser and beloved friend. Sometimes this faithful servant of the Lord had to tell hard things to the king, but even then Nebuchadnezzar did not blame Daniel. Once it was by very painful ways that this great ruler was brought to know the one true God, but in the end he worshipped Him, and humbly owned that he held his mighty kingdom in the power of the Lord Jehovah.

When Nebuchadnezzar died his son Belshazzar became king. He cared for nothing but pleasure and feasting, and had no use for his father's wise advisers.

Belshazzar the king made a great feast to a thousand of his lords.

While they were all feasting riotously, the king ordered the gold and silver vessels which his father had taken from the Temple in Jerusalem to be brought in. These sacred vessels were then filled with wine, and to shouts of scornful laughter, Belshazzar and his guests drank, and praised their heathen gods.

In that very moment there came the fingers of a man's hand and wrote on the plaster of the wall, just where the candlesticks lit it up. And the king saw the part of the hand that wrote

The noisy laughter was hushed, and the revellers watched in silence as the fingers traced four words—

MENE, MENE, TEKEL, UPHARSIN. Then the hand vanished.

The king shook with fright, and that great assembly sat as if turned to stone.

Then Belshazzar shouted, " Fetch my magicians and wise men. Whoever can read this writing, and tell its meaning, shall be clothed in purple, and have a gold chain about his neck. He shall be the third ruler in the kingdom."

The wise men came—but none of them could even read the writing.

The king grew more and more terrified!

Then the queen said:

" Do not be troubled, O king. There is a man in your kingdom who was the trusted friend of your father. He can interpret dreams and strange sayings."

" Let Daniel be called. He will tell you the meaning of the writing. The Spirit of his God is in him."

So Daniel was brought in, and Bel-shazzar told him what he had promised to the one who could read the writing and show its meaning.

Daniel spoke sternly to the frightened king.

" I do not want your gifts," he said. " I will do as you ask—but I warn you !—your father learned that the Most High God rules in the kingdom of men, and that He alone is the One who sets up kings."

" You knew this, but you have not cared. You have lifted up yourself against Him, and have drunk wine to heathen gods in the sacred vessels of His Temple."

" That is why He has sent the hand, and inscribed the writing."

" Now I will read it, and tell you what it means."

First Daniel read aloud the words so clearly printed on the wall but now the last word had changed:

MENE, MENE, TEKEL, PERES.

Then sadly, but truthfully, he told the meaning.

MENE—God has numbered your kingdom and finished it.

TEKEL—You are weighed in the balances and found wanting.

PERES—Your kingdom is divided, and given to the Medes and Persians.

Thus a wicked, pleasure-loving king heard God's judgment upon him. He was distressed and full of fear, but for once he acted fairly and justly. He insisted on rewarding Daniel with all the honours he had promised.

But that very night Belshazzar was slain, for Darius the Mede attacked the city of Babylon and captured it.

And Darius became king.

. . . . . .

Darius was a wise and thoughtful man, and at once began to make plans for ruling his kingdom well.

He divided it into provinces and chose one hundred and twenty princes as governors to look after them. Over these he set three presidents, and Daniel was one of them.

But this new king soon realized that, of all his advisers, Daniel was the wisest and the best. He could be trusted above everyone because of his calm and steadfast spirit.

So Darius began to think of setting Daniel over the other presidents and making him second only to himself.

The other presidents and the princes were furiously angry and jealous. Why should this man of a captive people rule over them!

" We must get rid of him," they said.

Then these men who hated Daniel began to watch him.

" If we can only find him doing something wrong," they whispered to each other, " we can tell the king tales about him."

They watched and waited, but never could they find a fault. Daniel was true and just even in the smallest thing, and carried out the king's business faithfully and well.

" It is no good," his enemies said at last. " We shall find no fault in this Daniel unless we can find it in something which touches the law of his God. What can we do? "

They talked it over, and together they made a cruel and wicked plan.

Then the other two presidents, with the princes and governors, went eagerly to the palace to see the king.

"O king Darius, live for ever," they said, as they bowed before him. "We and all your counsellors and governors have been talking together and want you to make a royal law, that whoever shall pray or ask anything of any god or man for thirty days, except of you, O king, shall be cast into the den of lions."

"We ask you to sign the writing so that it cannot be changed. It shall be as the law of the Medes and Persians which cannot be altered."

The king was rather pleased and proud to make a law that gave him such glory.

So he signed the writing, and forbade his people for thirty days to offer any prayer, or ask anything of any god or man but himself.

Then the presidents and princes went away satisfied. They felt that now this captive Jew they hated would soon be destroyed.

Again they watched and waited!

Now Daniel knew that the law was made and the writing signed, and that to disobey meant death.

But he served the Lord Jehovah. He could never pray, except to Him, the one true God.

So calmly and fearlessly he did as he had always done. Three times a day he opened the windows of his room which looked towards Jerusalem, the beloved royal city of the Jews, and he kneeled upon his knees and prayed, and gave thanks before his God.

And the men who watched with such cruel eagerness saw what he did!

That was the moment for which they had been waiting. They rushed to the palace and they could hardly hide their triumphant joy when they stood before the king.

" O king Darius," they said, " have you not made a law that anyone who shall ask anything for thirty days, except from you, O king, shall be cast into the den of lions? "

" Yes," the king answered, " that is true. It is a law like that of the Medes and Persians which cannot be altered."

Quickly one of the presidents told his tale.

" That Daniel, who is one of the captives of Judah, takes no heed of you, O king, nor of the law you have made. He prays to his own God three times a day. He openly disobeys you! "

As he looked at the dark, evil faces of the men who waited in grim silence to see what he would say, king Darius realized that he had been trapped by a cruel plot.

He was terribly upset. What could he do to save the man he loved and trusted?

He thought and worried for hours—but the presidents and princes meant to destroy Daniel.

" Know, O king," they said, " that no law you have made can be altered. It must be obeyed."

Sadly the king agreed. He gave orders, and Daniel was brought before him to be cast into the den of lions. One gleam of hope Darius had as he spoke pleadingly to the bound, helpless prisoner:

" Your God whom you serve so faithfully will surely save you."

Daniel was thrown into the lions' den, and a great stone was laid upon its opening, shutting him in with the fierce, hungry animals. Then the king sealed the stone with his own signet, and some of the nobles put their seals upon it, so that no one could move the stone and try to save Daniel.

Then those cruel men went away rejoicing that they had got rid of the Jew they envied and hated.

But king Darius went back to his palace almost broken-hearted. He would not eat, and he would not let his musicians play before him. All that night he did not sleep, but spent the long dark hours in sorrow and mourning.

What trouble his foolish pride had brought upon him!

Very early in the morning, at the first gleam of light, king Darius got up and hurried from the palace. Quickly he ran along the shadowy path which led to the lions' den, and, hardly daring to hope, he cried out in a sorrowful voice:

"O Daniel, servant of the living God, is your God whom you serve so faithfully able to deliver you from the lions?"

Then joyfully and triumphantly came the answer:

"O king, live for ever. My God has sent His angel and shut the lions' mouths, because I had done no wrong, nor any hurt to you, O king."

How glad and thankful Darius felt! He made haste to order his servants to break the seals, and to take up Daniel out of the den.

Daniel stood before the king, and those who saw this wonderful thing were amazed that the lions had not even hurt him. The God in whom he trusted had saved His servant.

Afterwards Darius made sure that those cruel presidents and princes were punished.

Then the king made a new law, which was proclaimed throughout all his empire.

" Peace be unto you! "

" I make a decree that, in all my dominions, men fear the God of Daniel. He is the living God, and steadfast for ever."

So through Daniel's firm, brave faith, Darius and his people were led to honour the one true God.

Now the king made this beloved Jew the second ruler in his kingdom, and God blessed Daniel, and gave him wisdom and understanding.

Series 522